Richard J. Levis

Diary of a Spring Holiday in Cuba

Richard J. Levis

Diary of a Spring Holiday in Cuba

ISBN/EAN: 9783337184551

Printed in Europe, USA, Canada, Australia, Japan

Cover: Foto ©Raphael Reischuk / pixelio.de

More available books at **www.hansebooks.com**

DIARY

OF A

Spring Holiday

IN

CUBA.

PHILADELPHIA:

PORTER & COATES.

1872.

TO

THOSE WHO WILL BE, FOR MY SAKE,

ITS MOST INTERESTED READERS,

My Aged Parents,

THIS SIMPLE RECORD OF TROPICAL WANDERING

IS AFFECTIONATELY

INSCRIBED.

DIARY

OF A

Spring Holiday in Cuba.

STEAMSHIP JUNIATA,
AT SEA OFF THE CAPES OF DELAWARE BAY,
Saturday Evening, Feb. 24th, 1872.

BOUND for a land of perpetual summer, we take a farewell backward look at the dark and frowning sky of winter. A cold gray mist blurs the outline of the ice-bound shores, where the black gulls of winter flap their broad wings over the surf. A chill north wind blows, but it only hastens us southward toward sunlit seas and radiant skies. The last glimpse of the dim shore of homeland fades away, and our thoughts turn, as the prow of the vessel points, to the warm and genial South

1*

Sunday, February 25th.—Sailors have a traditional saying, that there is "no Sunday beyond five fathoms soundings," and it is apparent that the day has no formal characteristic
at sea.

The wind is light, and the waves give us but a
gentle swaying motion; yet it is enough to keep
our fellow-passengers in their state-rooms, on account of sea-sickness. So the day passes quietly
away, while we gradually become accustomed to
the new surroundings of sight, sound, and motion; the deep respiration of the steam-exhaust,
the pulsating throbs and heavy strokes of the
engine, sending a tremor through the frame of
this great sea monster; the solemn tone of the
ship's bell, repeated every half hour; and, to us,
a bell, increasing hourly in attractions, which
calls us to the well-spread cabin table. The sea
continues so quiet that there would seem to be
no cause for sea-sickness, but the captain states
that the ailment is much under the influence
of the imagination, as passengers often repeat
the inquiry as to whether we are "outside yet,"

and on being answered in the affirmative, retire to their state-rooms and go through the formalities.

Yet there must be a miserable reality in sea-sickness, which requires great resignation to bear it patiently. A gentleman, whose histrionic fame is known to every one, being at sea and suffering from sea-sickness, which he bore with extreme impatience, a fellow-passenger strove to console him with the example of other and more resigned sufferers, and even alluded to the Saviour's being at sea in a tempest. The petulant invalid replied: "That is so; but, if my memory is not at fault, he got out and walked! and I cannot do that."

This starting out to sea reminds me of my only previous experience, in a time long ago, when with feelings different indeed I first saw the ocean's expanse. I recall vividly, but with a shade of sadness, an affectionate parting on starting off, youthful, buoyant, and careless. Then life seemed an endless morning, and the vista an unlimited horizon. The present voyaging seems

as but a mid-day rest in a toilsome way; or, perhaps, with the day, it may be, far spent, when I
should be looking trustingly forward as being

> "Nearer to the wayside inn,
> Where toil shall cease and rest begin."

Of one of that little home-circle there is nothing
left but her memory; the snow of this parting
winter is melting on the marble that encloses her,
and the slanting rays of a glowing winter sunset
are smiling over her repose.

Tuesday, February 27*th.*—If the " three wise
men of Gotham," of infantile literature, who
" went to sea in a bowl," had chosen this aus-
picious time their story would have been longer.
The sea continues as the quiet surface of a mill-
pond; even the traditional stormy locality of
" off Cape Hatteras," is passed without wind or
waves. The sun shines warmly, the sky is a deep
blue, and the air is like the balmy breath of June.
This transition from the cheerless breaking up
of winter, from fields of floating ice to the drift-

ing seaweeds of the warm waters of the Gulf Stream, is exceedingly grateful.

Thursday, February 29th.—The sea has still an unruffled surface, and evidences of the tropical change are increasing; the sun comes up red from its hot-bath in the gulf waters, and glows in a cloudless sky until it dips again in the crimson west.

There is a tranquilizing influence in this warm sea air of the South, which tends to mental repose and an idle and dreamy existence. It is occupation enough to lie on deck and gaze on the blue expanse; to watch the heavy flight of the pelicans, the wayward flapping of the gulls, the antics of the flying-fish, or the wind-borne fleets of nautilus.

The vessel has been since yesterday morning running along the coast of Florida, near enough to discern persons, if any existed on that barren strand; but with the exception of several lonely light-houses, and, in the evening, some Indian camp-fires, no signs of human life were seen.

Some wrecked vessels loom up as ghostly warn-

ings on the beach, where their skeletons will long
bleach in the sun and spray; and we but recently
passed the spot where the very steamship we are
on was cast, a helpless waif, in the great hurricane
of last August. The vessel, while endeavoring
with all the power of steam to keep away from the
shore, head to the wind, was hurled backward and
struck the sand; when to save life she was headed
directly for the strand, and went flying before
the blast up among the trees on the beach. No
damage was sustained, and in a few days she was
again on her way.

We have a winged visitor from the ever-
glades of Florida. A little weary wanderer, with
bright yellow and brown plumage, has found
rest on the vessel, and is cared for in the pilot-
house, to be set at liberty when we reach the
harbor.

Friday, March 1st. — It was announced last
evening that the light-house on Morro Castle
would soon be in sight, but as no vessel is per-
mitted to enter the harbor after the firing of the
gun at sunset, or before the gun at sunrise, the

ship steamed slowly onward, so as not to be too early at the entrance of the harbor.

At daybreak a black and threatening horizon, with gusty squalls, hid the island from view; but as it gradually broke away, the distant mountains came in sight, and the bright sunlight soon displayed the promised land—the land of the cocoa and the palm, of my childhood's dreams of tropic fruits and gorgeous flowers, of waving cane-fields, burning suns, and toiling slaves!

A signal sent to the top of the flagstaff on Morro Castle announced our arrival in Havana, and we passed through the very narrow entrance of the harbor, almost under the guns, and within talking distance of the sentinel in white and red, and burnished trappings, who paced the parapet. The castle has a most grand and romantic appearance, overhanging the sea at a great eminence, its high walls crested by rows of cannon, surmounted at one angle by a towering lighthouse; its base washed by the warm waters of the Gulf Stream, and lashed by its foaming surf. It impressed me more, however, with the idea of romance than of power, and it seemed that its chalky stone could soon be made to crumble under modern projectiles, and its guns be tumbled into the sea. In addition to the Morro, there are several other fortifications, which, although not so picturesque, are probably of greater strength; and the harbor, on account of its narrow entrance, with high surrounding hills, must be naturally one of the most readily defensible in the world.

The city, until this moment partially hidden from view by the castle and hills at the harbor's entrance, now spread suddenly out, its light-colored buildings of yellow and blue tints dazzling in the morning sun. The harbor was filled with vessels, not at wharves, but dispersed at their anchorages, including war ships of every maritime nation, decked with their national flags; and more conspicuous than all others, the Russian fleet, which had just arrived with the Grand Duke, on his visit to the island.

As we came along the harbor, a curious scene, which may be witnessed every day, was that of a hundred or more horses from the city, led into the water in droves by their drivers, taking a morning bath in the surf. The surrounding country seemed rather bare of foliage but clothed in deep green, and that most prominent of all tropical characteristics, the royal palm tree, with its long, straight, and bare trunk stretching high in the air, its feathery top waving in the wind, was in every direction seen.

In addition to the varied novelties of sight, were those of sound; for a most extraordinary ringing of bells resounded from the city, as if it were some hour of jubilee, but I was informed that all this wrangle and jangle was only the calling of the devout to their matins. The sounds were neither musical nor inspiring, no deep-toned resonance, but a most discordant twanging, as if of hundreds of colossal cow-bells in towers and steeples.

The harbor was alive with little, active, light-colored boats, with a framework and awning stretched over the stern portion, like a wagon-cover, to protect from the sun. From one of these

2

a pilot came on board, and conducted the vessel
to her moorings; from others came the custom-
house officials; and in one was seen by us the
welcome sight of the kind face of a friend who,
anticipating our arrival, had come out to greet us
and guide our way through the formalities prior
to landing. We gathered ourselves and baggage
into one of these boats, and proceeded to the
custom-house, where the trunks were unlocked
in anticipation of a great overturning and scrutinizing search of their contents; but we must
have been honored in the breach of this custom,
for the official merely poked his long and spec-
tacled nose under the trunk lids, as if to smell
rather than to see, and placing a chalk-mark on
them, which in our vernacular would, I suppose,
be written " O K," the trunks were passed out.

Then came our funny experience of the place;
the strange-looking jail-like houses, with barred
windows without sash or glass; the large heavily-
ironed doors; the narrow and crowded streets without sidewalks, and the motley crowds of varied
dress, complexion, and nationality, who jabbered,

jostled, laughed, and quarreled in their way.
The oddity of vehicles is the most striking of all
things to a stranger, including the awkward and

VOLANTE DRIVER.

ungainly volante, with one horse in the long
shafts, and another in traces alongside, mounted
by a negro in gaudy trappings, red jacket,
leather leggings, slippers, and enormous spurs.

Our destination was the San Carlos, or the
Hotel Telegrafo, but no accommodations could be
found in them, and we were quartered in the Hotel
de Santa Isabel, a house which looks as if it were
some decayed palace of royalty. Here are tiled

and marble floors throughout, above and below;
porcelain wainscots highly ornamented;—all this
grandeur, mingled with the utmost confusion of
broken furniture, baggage, scattered fruits and
vegetables; some doves flying in and out; un-

HOTEL SANTA ISABEL.

pleasant odors of kitchen and cookery, all redo-
lent of garlic; and other evidences of disorder,
and, to us, of discomfort. We sat down in our
curious room, overlooking on one side a court-
yard, where a dried-up fountain remained as an

ornament, the other window giving a view over
the bay; when our friend, who had so kindly
met us, loaded the table with a fragrant heap of
oranges and bananas, which were enjoyed as
tropical fruits can only be appreciated in perfection, in the land of their production.

After visiting a money changer, and turning
some of our national currency into Spanish gold,
I rode about the streets in a volante, observing
the curiosities of people and architecture, and
visited a restaurant to taste the peculiar forms of
refreshments.

The private houses look like castles for defence,
and the style of building has probably continued
from olden times, when it was essential that each
dwelling-house should be defensible from the In-
dians, and more especially from pirates, who have
often pillaged the towns on the coast.

The floors are all either stone or tile, the walls
are immensely thick, and the stone partitions of
the separate apartments continue up higher than
the roof, so that the space above it is divided into
distinct pens three or four feet high; thus a

series of battlement-walls, well suited for defence, exists on every house. There are no yards or gardens as we construct in our homes, but within the area of the house is a court-yard, open to the air and sun above, into which doors, and barred, unglazed windows, open from all the rooms. It is curious to see the volante, or other form of family carriage, driven apparently into the parlor or entry, and there remain as if it were a part of the parlor furniture; thus, on entering a handsome private residence, the first object seen is the volante, with its polished and showy silver or gold mountings, standing there an object of ornament and family pride. I saw no ladies to-day in the streets, but as I passed the barred windows, a view of the inner life of the Cuban family was readily obtained, for the windows reach the ground, and being without glass, the temptation to look in at the ladies was, of course, irresistible; and, when dressed for display, they present themselves for this kind of observation.

On returning to the hotel, our courteous friend proposed that we should accompany him to Ma-

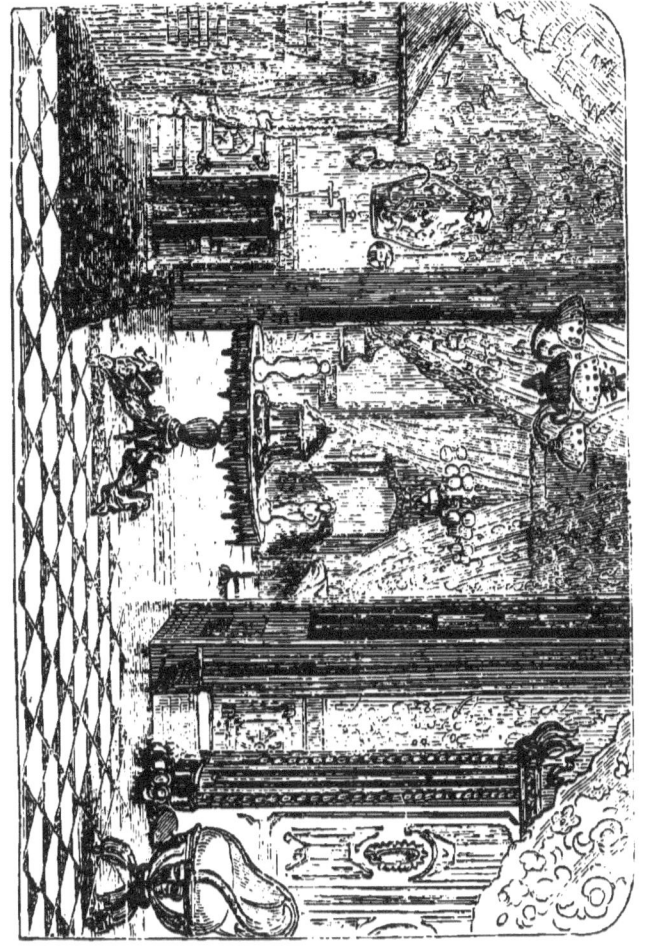

INTERIOR OF A CUBAN HOUSE.

tanzas, his place of residence; and being desirous
of having at once a rural view of the tropics,
the proposal was gladly acceded to; and this
decision was the more prompt after having been
introduced to an American gentleman at the
hotel, whose countenance resembled a skull with
lemon-colored parchment drawn over it, and who
was being congratulated by his friends on his re-
covery from yellow fever!

So we bade farewell to Santa Isabel, gathered ourselves into vehicles drawn by emaciated
ponies, who were lashed and spurred, as is the
custom, until the ferry to the railway station was
reached.

A steam ferry-boat, like those of the North,
crossed the bay to Regla, whence a railway train,
of American style, soon started for Matanzas,
going at very great speed.

The country was for some distance barren and
rocky, and, with the exception of the peculiar
tropical vegetation, did not differ from our northern waste lands. As the journey proceeded, the
country became more attractive; verdant and

waving cane-fields bordered the road, large tracts
of banana plants, weighed down by their heavy
branches of the fruit, and groves of orange trees
were on every side; and above all and ever in
sight was the tall and graceful royal palm, with
its straight light-colored trunk, surmounted by
its waving tuft of fern-like leaves, the most beautiful of nature's forest productions.

The country is evidently rendered bare by the
destruction of the forests for fuel, but the gorgeous palm is alone spared in the devastation,
and remains an object of ornament and utility,
so that it is seen cresting every hill-top, and in
groves on the plains.

Before reaching Matanzas, its surrounding
mountains, which are familiar landmarks from
far out on the ocean, were seen, and soon we
were among the variegated blue and yellow buildings of the environs of the city.

Located at the Hotel Leon de Oro, the singu-
larities of Cuban life become the subject of observation; and on entering we are impressed at
once with the savors of cookery, including, of

course, the prominent flavor of garlic; for the culinary arrangements are immediately under our eyes, and, unfortunately, under our nose also. The dinner was soon served, made up of varied familiar articles disguised into strangeness, and some unfamiliar ones in which tasting could not solve the problem, and which would have needed the services of an interpreter for comprehension; but it finished off, as is the cutsom, with the odd combination of guava jelly and strong cheese, and an abundance of fruits.

Our room holds two beds conveniently, and has the invariable tiled floor, and the ceiling is at a great elevation, probably nearly thirty feet; but the beds, so called, are merely sacking-bottoms stretched at great tension, and resemble in every respect the head of a drum. Such is a Cuban bed for all of high or low degree, and it may do for those whose bones and integument are not too near together, but as only the salient points of the body can touch it, the arrangement seems more calculated for the production of aching backs and bed-sores, than for repose. The pillows are very small, inelastic, and sodden, as if filled with dough.

Sunday, March 3d.—Matanzas differs from Havana in being much smaller, but has the same characteristics of narrow streets, massive low stone houses, and retains even more of the ancient Moorish peculiarities.

Like other Spanish cities it has its grand plaza, where the higher classes throng in the evenings to see and to be seen, and to listen to the music of the military bands, the ladies sitting languidly in their volantes, while the gentlemen promenade about the walks, saluting them in the complimentary and fulsome fashion of the country.

I have been expecting to see the population with their faces tinged with the livery of the burning sun, but have been impressed with the pallid and anæmic countenances of most of the people, particularly the ladies, and the men of the higher classes. Our own party really look, according to my ideal, more Spanish than the Spaniards. None but the laboring people expose

themselves to the sun's rays, and there is prevalent a most indolent aversion to bodily exercise;
and the ladies flit out only in a moth-like existence when the shades of evening veil them. No
ruddy cheeks are seen, no lithe forms and brisk
tripping feet patter on the pavements as in the
North; but the Cuban belle, with her dark languishing eyes, placid, dignified countenance, profuse black hair, and dressed in some lace-like
tissue, ventures out only in her volante, and re-
clines languidly on her cushions for the evening
drive on the paseo or plaza.

There are many showy stores, at least in their
inside display, for the goods are not arranged in
windows, which are merely heavily barred grat-
ings without glass; and the fronts of even the
best stores have a most forbidding appearance.
They are invariably attended by males, and the
same sex seem to be almost the exclusive visitors. When the ladies go out to do their shop-
ping it is in their volantes, which they do not
leave to enter the stores, but the goods are
brought out and displayed to them by the very

3

attentive and polite clerks. Some of the stores are distinguished by remarkable appellations assumed for them by their proprietors, and painted on signs, many of which are singular for their oddity and inappropriateness. Thus the titles of a few of the quaintest when translated are: My Recreation; My Pleasure, Sweet Name of Jesus; Son of the Town; Poor Devil; Rich Devil; and others are called the Green Cross; Hope; Oriental; Norma, etc. Funny attempts at translating are noticeable on store signs, to make the business comprehensible to foreigners; such an one is, "Joni sel her," which intends to say, "Honey sold here!"

It is curious to observe the manner in which the daily supply of vegetables and market commodities comes into the city, all on the backs of horses and mules, whose bodies are often almost entirely hidden under their bulky loads of packs and panniers. This is particularly so with the animals laden with almost a stack of green corn-fodder, when only the nose can be seen projecting from the moving mass, and only the clatter of hoofs heard beneath. Trains of burdened mules and horses come into the town in long processions, single file, being kept in line by each one's head being tied to the tail of the one in front of him.

There is heard here the same unmelodious ringing of bells which saluted us on disembarkation; it is the same tin-pan sound, commencing at daybreak, and reiterated at intervals until the vesper hour relieves us of the noisy jargon. Notwithstanding all this noisy summoning, on visiting the ancient cathedral at the hour of evening prayers, I found but three persons in the sombre and dimly lighted hall, kneeling devoutly and in silence before the crucifixes.

As the visit of the Russian prince is expected for to-morrow, preparations are being made to receive him, including the putting in order of some streets through which he will pass, and for this purpose the chain-gang, composed of convicted criminals, chained in pairs by the waist and by one leg, is actively at work under the control of an armed guard.

I have returned this evening from a most interesting sailing expedition down the bay of Matanzas and up the Canimar River. The water of
the bay is of a bright blue color, such as we see in
Italian marine pictures, excepting in the shoaler
places, where an emerald green blends beautifully
with it. A stiff breeze was blowing, and the
mouth of the river was soon reached, passing a
little fort mounting two guns, located at the entrance of the channel, and formerly used to keep
slave-traders from harboring there. The river is
narrow but deep, and its scenery is of the most
rugged and romantic character. Its rocky sides
are higher, and more broken and precipitous than
those of the Wissahickon, and are clad with the
gorgeous and enormous tropical vegetation. The
tall royal palms majestically top off the rocky
crests, and smaller varieties of the palm, and the
fan-leaved palmettos, spring forth wherever they
can get a lodgment for their roots in the rocks.

A remarkable and beautiful effect is produced
by the orchids, and other varieties of air plants
which are conspicuous on every large tree. Some

trees are conspicuous only by the orchids which fasten on them at every bifurcation of branches, and large, entirely dead trees are in appearance resurrected to vernal life by the enormous growth of these parasites. The night-blooming cereus is ever in sight, and the maguey or century plant is now in its gorgeous bloom of reddish-yellow, at the top of stems sometimes twenty feet high, with masses of flowers, one to two feet or more in diameter.

The rugged rocky cliffs which border the stream are evidently upheavals of coral and shell formations, and are even at their tops composed of marine fossils. They have an eroded or water-worn appearance, and large caverns exist in them, which in their dark recesses have for ages been the homes of vast numbers of bats. The floors of these caves are deeply covered with a guano-like material, deposited by the bats, and in one locality it was attempted to make a commercial article of it, but it is said without success. I saw no evidence of stratification of the rocks, excepting at the mouth of the river.

Tracts of bamboo on small, low, or level places, and many plants of exuberant tropical growth, but unknown to me. varied the vegetation on the banks. The only birds I saw were pelicans and herons, and some varieties of small birds with brilliant yellow and black plumage. An interesting visit was made to a country store, at a rope ferry across the river, where the people, Sunday as it was, were gathered for purchases, and for drinking spirits. The store was filled with the varied commodities required by this peculiar community, and among those in demand was what I at first thought to be sole-leather, but it proved to be meat, salted and dried in the sun, called jerked beef, and which is the only form that meat usually reaches the laborers. On returning at night a chilling north wind was blowing, and, weary with the day's excitement and exertion, with appetites sharpened, we returned to our— garlic, and found as much repose as could be obtained on our drum-head couches.

Tuesday, March 5th.—Last evening we visited socially by invitation the residence of a friend, and had the pleasure of meeting a gathering of Cuban ladies and gentlemen, some of whom could speak our language. The residence is a fair specimen of the general style of dwellings of the refined classes, of one story, the roof being high but flat, and covered with tiles. The windows reach

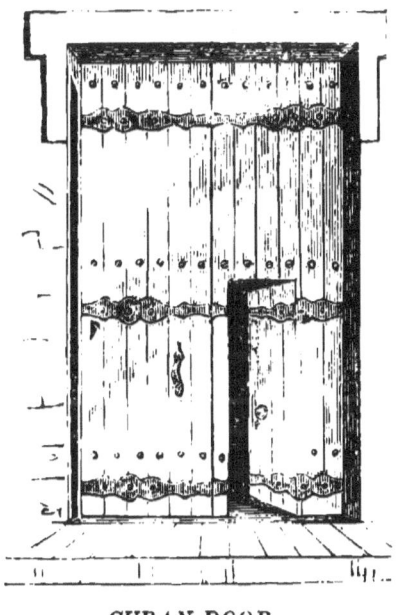

CUBAN DOOR.

almost from the floor to the ceiling, and have the invariable jail-like iron grating instead of glazed sashes. The front door is as heavy and strong as that of a prison, and is ornamented with heavy

metallic castings, and has great locks and bolts.
The family carriage is driven through this door,
and when not in use, remains in the hall, within
observation from the principal rooms.

The rocking-chair is a feature in the Cuban
parlor, and the other chairs are formed for loung-
ing and repose. Rocking-chairs are arranged
facing each other in rows, and the company sit
in these formal lines, but in quite social proximity.

Refreshments in the form of chocolate, coffee,
and cakes, were served during the evening, and
were agreeable.

The remarkable subterranean caves of Bellamar
are in the neighborhood of Matanzas, and were
the subject of an interesting visit this morning.
Volantes were ordered, and we went off at a dash-
ing pace along the side of the bay, the blue and
emerald waters glittering in the morning sun;
and when we arose to some elevation, overlooking
the water, the transparency was apparent, show-
ing the white, shelly bottom at considerable
depth. On this ride was first demonstrated to

me the real and essential merits of the volante, with its enormous wheels and long springing shafts. The road was rocky, with deep ruts and steep hills, yet the vehicle, with its two horses, one in the shafts and another in traces, mounted by the driver, went springing and swaying along over obstructions that would have wrecked an ordinary carriage.

The entrance of the cave is a perpendicular opening on level but elevated ground, overlooking the bay and ocean. On alighting from the volante, one of the drivers climbed a cocoanut-palm tree, and threw down some of the nuts, from which we were refreshed by cool draughts of the water contained in them. A portion of the green covering of the nut is cut off, and a pint or more of water, with the peculiar flavor of the nut, is a ready and agreeable drink.

Before entering the cave, it was essential to remove superfluous clothing, as the air within is very warm and damp. Descending a flight of steps, a hall of splendor was seen, of pure whiteness, overhung with drooping stalactites, all glittering, their crystalline surfaces reflecting the light from two wax candles, which we followed through the intricate and dark passages. The interior varied from narrow and low-roofed paths to lofty chambers, everywhere lined with dazzling white crystals in gothic arches, arborescent hangings, and other fantastic forms.

Some pools of clear water, and deep, dangerous-looking chasms were seen. We wandered through this labyrinth for a mile and a half, and then turned on a backward course along other avenues of interest and beauty. The sight of a glimmer of daylight was welcome when the wandering was near its end, and, with red faces and dripping with perspiration, we enjoyed again the fresh air on emerging from the cave. On our way, some fair specimens of the crystalline and stalactite formation were picked up, to be retained as mementoes of this wonder of nature, which is said to exceed in beauty all other caves in the world.

This evening we are packing up for an early start for the interior of the island to visit, by special invitation, the sugar plantation of Santa Barbara, located about sixty miles distant. In leaving the Hotel Leon de Oro, it will be with a knowledge that, notwithstanding its discomforts and oddities to us, it is commended as one of the best in the country. With its marble floors, open and airy halls, courteous attendants, and the liberality of its table, we have been pleased; while we have also been pleased to laugh over its quaint and disorderly accumulation of old furniture, like the contents of an antique garret; the curious and out-of-place position of everything useful and useless; and, while indulging deeply in the many really good and novel dishes before us, have taken the privilege of turning up our noses at its compounds of garlic and oil. Its total absence of the female sex for attendants—not a woman being seen in the house—and the substitution of Chinese masculines for cooks, waiters, washerwomen, and for the ordinary duties of a chambermaid, seems very funny, especially so when they carry coffee at early morning to the ladies, still in dishabille, or shrinking under the sheets. Of its lively little parasites, in the form of fleas, I will find no fault until time allows me to know whether it be, as is reported, that the insect is ubiquitous in the island. However, of its enormous cockroaches, I have one word to say; they are of the most aristocratic kind—at least, they are big bugs!

In leaving Matanzas, it will be with the recognition of our indebtedness to the good people who, though we were strangers, met us with outstretched arms, led us to their homes, and made us gratefully to know that the tradition of Cuban hospitality is not a myth, but a reality which must leave its impress so long as memory shall last.

Wednesday, March 6th.—With delightful anticipations of visiting a sugar plantation, in the early morning we saw, from our balcony windows, the volantes ready, and were speedily whirled away to the station of the railroad, which leads in a southeasterly direction to the interior of the island. In the first-class car we found but few passengers, and before the end of the journey was reached, our party were its sole occupants; but the second and third classes were well filled. The three grades of cars did not seem to differ materially in the style of accommodations; all that I noticed was that the first class have cane seats and backs, whilst those of the inferior rate were simply wooden; yet the general difference of caste of the three classes of travelers was apparent.

Whenever the train was about to start from a station, a Chinese attendant walked along the platform jingling a hand-bell—for bells seem indeed in favor in this country—and soon off went the train without anything like our familiar, "All right!" or, "Go ahead!"

The morning was bright and pleasant, and the air invigorating; but our fellow-travellers did not seem to so appreciate it, for our windows were the only ones opened; and there they sat, whilst the smoke of the omnipresent cigar gathered densely around them. At every station a couple' of soldiers, in blue linen with red trimmings, entered the train and walked through in a scrutinizing

4

manner. At these stopping-places were stands for selling refreshments to travelers, such as cakes, guava jelly, cheese, and fruit; but the ones most patronized were those which dealt out the usual alcoholic beverage—a kind of rum made from the sugar-cane.

As the interior of the country was reached, the resemblance of the level ground to our western prairies impressed me. The soil is deep and rich, generally of a red-chalk color, but sometimes almost black, and the profusion of tropical vegetation increased as the journey proceeded.

In the midst of a region of sugar plantations, indicated in the distance by the towering chimneys of the sugar mills, we were set down from the train, and found a volante and saddle horses kindly sent for us from the plantation of Santa Barbara.

As I sit down now to write at this tropical Eden, with bloom and fruit and the sweet harvest of the cane around; with the glowing sun dipping behind the distant palm trees and casting their long shadows on the heated earth, I

can well understand the enthusiasm which Columbus, the great discoverer of the Island, felt

COUNTRY GARDEN.

when, addressing his sovereign, he wrote: "This
is the most beautiful land eyes ever beheld."

Friday, March 8th.—A Cuban bed is conducive to early rising. By the time your angularities give you the sensation of lying on a gridiron, turning hopelessly over and over again to find a soft spot; when your ears ache from compression on the hard pillows, and you are tired of amusing yourself by drumming a tattoo with your fingers on the tense sacking-bottom, then a streak of daylight in the dappled east is welcome.

The Cuban habit of taking coffee on rising, with or before the sun, and then starting off for the morning ride, returning for a late breakfast, is an agreeable practice in this region, where exposure to the mid-day sun is oppressive. The horses were ready saddled at the door this morning as we sipped our coffee, just as the stars grew pale and the mist lightened up to the eastward. The heavy dew matted down the grass, and the long leaves of the sugar cane drooped and dripped with excess of moisture.

Our way led by the endless cane fields, through groves of palms, and brushed through the broad-leaved patches of bananas, until a stream of water was reached, in which some beautiful wood-ducks paddled away into the seclusion of a thicket over-hanging the bank.   Along the edge of the forest, too dense to penetrate, the singing birds, always most musical at early hours, mingled their, to my ears, unfamiliar notes.

I plucked some sour wild oranges, for they looked too pretty to pass by as they shone in bright yellow contrast to the deep green leaves, and were plentiful within reach as we rode under the trees.   As soon as the sun gets a little eleva-tion, with the aid of the strong winds that arise with it, the dew is gone, and before we reached home, at the late breakfast hour, the pathway was already dusty.

Sunday, March 10th.—An early ride yesterday morning, gave a view of some of the agricultural processes of the plantation, for this season is an active period of the sugar-cane harvest.   At this early hour the laden ox-carts were returning from the field, for the laborers had been at work, as is the practice, since daylight, and the

4*

rude monotonous song of the cane gatherers could be heard from a distance.

Before nearing the field, the polished cutting-blades could be seen flashing in the morning sun.

SUGAR-CANE.

The cane cutters were in long line, each armed with a broad sword-like blade, wide and square at the end, and about two feet in length. Each

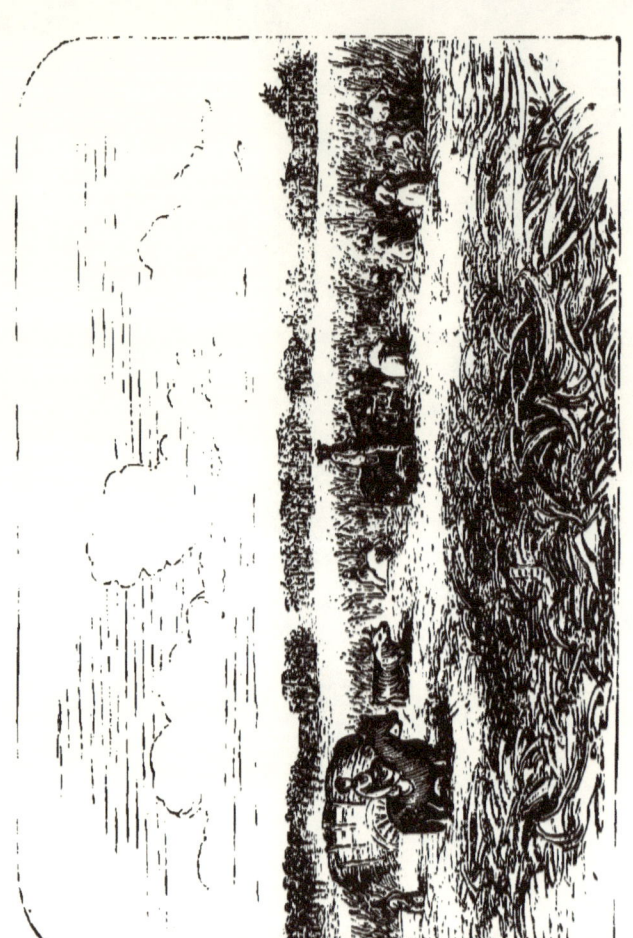

CUTTING SUGAR-CANE.

stalk of cane is seized in the hand and cut separately, one swing of the knife cutting off the
spreading leafy top, and another cut severing the
cane near to the ground.   As the stalks are cut,
they are thrown into rows to be picked up by the
gatherers with the ox-carts, the green tops being
left on the field to be eaten by the cattle.   The
troop of laborers was made up of negroes, a few
of whom were women, and of some Chinese, or
coolies, as they are called.

It seemed as if some mechanical substitute
might be made to relieve all this hand labor of
such large forces of workers, and do it much
more rapidly and cheaply, such as a large reap-
ing machine.   But the difficulty is, perhaps, in
the necessity for each stalk to be cut at least
twice, above and below; and also in some meas-
ure to the confused manner in which the canes
are massed together, some erect, others inclined
or entirely fallen.

The carts, with their shouting drivers and
three or four yokes of oxen, follow, and the cane
is piled into them, each holding two or three

tons; and when filled, they slowly move off
towards the crushing mill.

The oxen of these teams are smaller and more
tractable and intelligent, or under better training, than the oxen used in the North, being
obedient when each is separately called by name,
and some of the teams are under remarkable control by the voices of their drivers.

The drivers keep up a continued calling or
ordering the animals, in a tone that is not un-
musical, and I have been amused at the names of
the oxen, given to them by the negroes. Some of
the names which I heard this morning, when
translated, were, "Diamond," "Good Friend,"
"Dove," "Grain of Gold," "Poison," "Pretty,"
"Sailor," and "Runaway."

The laborers are directed in their field work by
an officer called the mayoral, who is the same in
authority as the slave driver of former times on
the plantations of our Southern States. He is an
ordinary sort of fellow, who merely knows the
work before him, and is mounted on a horse or
mule, and carries a sword and a large whip. The

CANE CARTS RETURNING.

use of the lash is forbidden by law, yet it is said to be often used; but I have not seen any instance of it on this plantation. It is, however, probable that the whip will of necessity be more or less used so long as slavery exists, as compulsion and the fear of punishment must be, in such hopeless servitude, the only incentives to work.

The punishment ordinarily resorted to, usually for criminal conduct, is confinement in the stocks and the wearing of chains. These forms of punishment simply detain or inconvenience the offender without inflicting pain.

The breakfast for the laborers was brought to the field about eight o'clock, and consisted of boiled jerked beef and boiled sweet potatoes, in a large wooden box or trough. Folding some cane leaves into a sort of basin, each laborer supplied himself liberally with the food, and sitting in the shade of the uncut cane, ate large quantities. This diet is varied at other meals with the plantain and rice, with sugar and water for a drink; and at all moments of idleness the negroes are seen gnawing and sucking the sugar-cane.

5

It is said that during the sugar-making season, notwithstanding the hard work, the laborers and working animals all become fat, due to the consumption of sugar or the cane. I have seen horses and dogs eat sugar, hogs and chickens fatten on the refuse of the mills, and flocks of birds feed on it where it is exposed in the sun and air to dry.

In case of heavy rains, particularly during the wet season, the laborers are protected by large sheds mounted on wheels, which are moved from place to place, and into which they gather until the heavy rain-fall is over.

Last evening was the occasion of great excitement on this plantation and the vicinity. On returning homeward, from our evening ride, there was a bright light in the horizon in front of us, but it did not attract much attention until it suddenly flared up, when, spurring our horses, it was soon seen that a cane-field was blazing and the fire rapidly extending.

This burning of cane-fields is the dread of the planter, and often the cause of great loss. On this plantation of Santa Barbara a fire once destroyed an amount of cane equivalent to two thousand boxes of sugar; and the blaze of cane-fields has extended over a continuous track of twenty miles, consuming property worth millions of dollars.

For the purpose of detecting fire in its incipiency, a watchman is, during the daytime, stationed in the cupola of the sugar-mill to strike an alarm.

Fire is most dreaded during the high winds that prevail from nine in the morning until five in the afternoon; the rest of the twenty-four hours being usually calm.

When we reached the cane-field the whole force of negroes and coolies was at work, some cutting a road through the field of cane at a distance in advance of the fire, so as to leave a space over which the fire could not advance, and others beating out newly ignited spots where sparks or coals were carried by the wind.

The heat was intense, and the stalks of green

cane, as they burst from expansion, kept up a sound like the rattle of distant musketry.

Fortunately the evening was of the usual calmness, and the vacated space where the cane had been cut and carried away before the fire, ended its progress.

Tuesday, March 12th.—My morning and evening rides always present some new object of interest; indeed the whole pathway is among beauties and novelties which create admiration and surprise. My recent transition from a climate of winter makes these impressions the more striking. The profuse bloom of tropical flowers, the most of which are to me unknown exotics, is always attractive; but there are among them some old familiar ones, such as the convolvulus with its blue and white or purple flowers, which are ever in sight, covering the hedges by the roadsides.

Many flowers are large and gaudy in color, among which the American aloe is very conspicuous, as long hedges are frequently formed of it, and the flower-stalks often reach to a height of twenty-five feet. Hedges are used for the partition of fields and to edge the roads, and many beautiful flowers peer out through the dense entanglement of the thicket.

The hedge is usually formed of a plant called the *piña raton*, which has long sword-like leaves edged with the sharpest points, and as it grows with rapidity and density, an impenetrable barrier is formed. The leaves are usually of a bright green color, but are curiously and beautifully varied, and some are a brilliant red.

Nothing in the way of vegetation has interested me as much as the parasites, which spread themselves over larger growths until they are completely enveloped. Some of these parasites become far larger than the object on which they at first effect a lodgment. The most remarkable to me is one which commences its growth up in the branches of a large tree and spreads itself; some of its offshoots descend and take root in the ground, and the tree is so entwined and enclosed by the parasite that it dies in the fatal embrace. Dead trees thus enclosed are abun-

5*

dantly seen in the forests; and where a large
tree has in this death-grasp been long dead it
may be decayed, and in time disappears, so that
sometimes this enormous growth of what was
once a mere parasite, now stands up alone with
the size, form, and firmness of the original tree.

I occasionally see dead trees covered with para-
sitic growths whose life is being again sapped
out by other vegetation upon them : " Thus death
takes the glow and hue of life, and life the gaunt
and ghastly form of death."

The density of these tropical forests is extreme, entangled as they are by intricate vines
hanging from aloft in festoons, and interwoven
with the drooping mosses, lichens, and small
undergrowth. In such places they can only be
penetrated, as is the custom, by cutting a way
with the short sword that is usually carried. In
the depth of these woods there is, on a calm day,
a grandeur and intense silence that produces a
feeling of awe.

Among the hanging vines of the forest is one
called the water vine, which has a curious utility.

When a piece of it is cut off, pure water flows rapidly in a stream from its porous wood, sufficient for the thirsty traveler, and I have several times had a cool and refreshing draught from a section of the vine. Some kinds of vines are long, smooth, and have a rope-like tenacity, and are used by the country people for tying fences and for bindings about their rudely constructed houses.

I have seen no animals in these forests except birds, snakes, and lizards; but an animal nearly the size of a rabbit, called the jutia, or wood rat, is abundant, and deer exist in some localities. Lizards vary in form, and are often beautifully colored. Snakes in this locality are not venomous, but some kinds, as the boa constrictor, are large. I have preserved the skin of one which living measured fifteen feet.

Thursday, March 14*th*.—This day has been one of great enjoyment, as it has been spent in a romantic picnic gathering of our social party in the woods.

After our cup of coffee at six in the morning,

and while the air was still fresh and cool, the foliage glittering with dew, a row of saddled horses and a volante were ready at the door. A mule cart with servants and provisions had preceded to make preparation for our breakfast at the encamping-ground.

The rising smoke from the fire, and when nearer, the savory aroma of roasted meat, led to an open grove by the side of a stream of water.

A whole pig was revolving and roasting over a fire of glowing coals, and was being attentively basted with orange-juice. The party amused themselves by wandering about, or by fishing in the stream, the ready fishing-poles being cut from bamboo growing on the bank, and with my gun I added a little to vary the fare with some game birds.

On returning to the grounds for breakfast, we found that a hungry party, sitting in silence aloft in the trees, had anticipated us. Flocks of turkey-buzzards had been seen, soaring high in the air, and were now in quiet dignity settled, like a coroner's jury at an inquest, over our roasting pig. They were harmless, and only aided in making the scene more picturesque.

A tablecloth was spread on the ground, and the breakfast was enjoyed as such fare, in the open air with its novel surroundings, always is.

A part of the bill of fare was to have been turtle soup, but this item was missing, as our only receipt for making the soup commenced with "first catch your turtle;" and this trifling preliminary was, after some efforts, decided to be a failure.

Some roamed while others dozed, the horses browsing on piles of sugar-cane tops cut for them, until the hour for departing homeward, when we left the spoils to a party of waiters dressed in black—the buzzards.

Their verdict, in these troublous times, will be an agreement that they, like other hungry Spanish officials, who are birds of a feather, will send in their bills, with clause added to report a *casus belli;* which, where the pig was eviscerated, will be an intestine war.

Saturday, March 16th.—So much life in the

open air, late and early, from the first glimmer of
dawn until the stars shine out and the glow-
worm marks the pathway, gives me a full appre-
ciation of this delightful climate. This is the
latter part of the dry season, for the word winter
is here unknown; but I anticipated that the dry
season would show a general desiccation and
withering, and am now surprised at the prevalent
verdure. Occasional showers have fallen throughout the season, and the country is of the bright
greenness of our "leafy month of June."

Some few trees, it is true, are bare of foliage,
and others merely budding forth; for even here,
" Leaves have their times to fall, and flowers to
wither," but not at the "north wind's breath."

The air is clear and pure, without much vari-
ation in temperature or moisture. The extremes
now are from seventy to ninety degrees, and the
average temperature of the island for the entire
year is eighty degrees. The sun's rays are hot
for exposure from 11 A.M. until 3 P.M.; before
and after those hours riding and walking are
agreeable.

All visiting, riding, and amusements out-of-doors are done in avoidance of the mid-day sun, yet the sunshine is quite tolerable to me, on account of the strong wind that almost invariably arises by nine or ten in the morning, and blows until four or five in the afternoon. I have not yet experienced a day that could be called sultry. The nights are calm and sufficiently cool for sleeping under blanket coverings.

The sky is clear and blue from sunrise until sunset, varied by white fleecy clouds, and the only rain, up to this date of my visit, has been an afternoon shower of an hour's duration.

The sunrises and sunsets are beautiful on account of the clearness of the atmosphere. At daylight there is a low mist on the ground, but as soon as the horizontal rays of the sun gleam over the tops of the distant palm-trees on the plain, it vanishes, and glowing sunlight reigns until the palms on the western horizon again cast forth their long shadows. The sun goes down red, and the clouds about are aglow with crimson and purple, but soon all is sombre evening, for there can hardly be said to be a period of twilight. The transition from day to night is rapid, and light drops into darkness as the curtain falls at the end of a performance, and an economical manager puts out the lights. The poetical hour of twilight, when "Fades the glimmering landscape on the sight," is lost in the intense tropical realities of sunshine and darkness. Thus, when riding at a distance from home, late in the day, I have been surprised by being quickly overtaken by the darkness.

The only marked change of temperature is during the dry season, when the wind blows from the north, which is not frequent or of long duration, but the air may then be chilly at night and early in the morning. This chilliness must at times, during the winter months, be uncomfortably felt by the people, as they universally wear linen clothing, and the beds, so-called, on which they sleep, cannot give warmth. It is not that the temperature actually falls so low, but the entire absence of all means of protection from coolness and dampness may produce discomfort, as

the houses are everywhere built to be cool and
airy, offering only shelter from sun and rain.
The houses throughout the rural localities are of
but one story, with tiled roofs, and usually floors
of stone or tiles.

The doors and windows open almost from floor
to ceiling. Windows are guarded only by iron
bars and heavy inside shutters, without any glass
sashes, and of course a chimney, or other arrangement for artificial warmth, is unknown in the
island. Thus it will be seen that the houses offer
no protection from a chilly atmosphere, and it is
certainly true that such protection is very rarely
needed; but I am prepared to advise every friend
who may be inclined to run away from winter,
and to experience this delightful climate, to bring
with him an overcoat for emergencies, and if he
should travel much through the beautiful interior, it would be well to be provided with his own
blanket, as he will find such articles scarce among
the country people.

The houses of the smaller farmers and the
country people generally, even among some who

are said to be wealthy, are of a character which we in the North would consider most wretched. But the wretchedness pertains to outward circumstances which do not exist in this tropical climate, where merely protection from sun and rain is desired. These houses are constructed of thin strips of the palm-tree or bamboo, with sometimes a fibrous material from the cocoanut tree packed in between them. The roof is thatched with palm leaves, and the floor merely the bare ground, and that is worn into a rough, uneven condition. There may be partitions dividing the space into several rooms, which seem usually dark on account of closure of the window-shutter, if there be one. A few rough chairs and a table constitute the furniture, which with some enormous and ornamented saddles, some ox-yokes, and a piece of jerked beef, with small sheafs of unhulled rice, or bunches of herbs hanging from the rafters, make up the household property.

I rode this morning through a country beyond the sugar plantations, among the poorer orders of

country people, who live in this style of houses.
They are an humble class, of marked peculiarities;
but their manners and courteous deportment in
general are their best features. Their dress is
primitive, being merely a linen shirt worn outside
the pantaloons, which are of the same material,
and a pair of low shoes or slippers on bare feet.
They continually wear swords, either long or
short, often ornamented with silver, and ride with
large rattling spurs. It is impossible to be among
them without being impressed with their kind-
ness, and, even among the humblest, with a little
polish of manner.

Monday, March 18*th.*—I have been wandering
to-day in some new directions, leaving the broad
plateau of the cane-fields, following streams of
water or the winding edges of the forest, and occasionally dismounting to penetrate the deep
shades and observe tropical nature in its seclusion and wildness.

It is interesting to see the peculiarities and the
exuberance of growth of trees and vines, but particularly the varieties of the parasites on trees, and

those particularly which we would call air-plants. There is great variety in the forest trees, the largest being the ceiba, some specimens of which are the greatest trees, both in height and size of trunk, that I have ever seen. There are trees which have the semblance of our larches, but the forest is almost made up of unfamiliar foliage.

The great tropical characteristic among trees is the royal palm, for it is the most conspicuous and most abundant of all. It is never out of sight, being spared in the clearing of forests; is cultivated in groves, and in long lines to form ornamental avenues; its branching top surmounts and waves over the smaller trees of the forest, and the horizon almost everywhere is a crest of palms. The tree has great utility; the outside hard incasement of the loose fibrous trunk is used as boards in building houses, and the branches serve for thatching. Near to the top of the tree, where the branches start out, is a material that is eaten on the table as a vegetable. It is a delicate and pure white substance, and I can attest its agreeableness as an article of diet, either boiled or raw. The palm has a long straight and bare trunk, reaching directly upward for even sixty or eighty feet. It has a smooth and clean grayish-white appearance, as if it had received a coat of whitewash, and my first sight of it, in the vicinity of dwellings, gave me the impression that such was the case.

Another tree of prominence and beauty is the cocoanut. It grows everywhere throughout the island, and is of utility for its fruit, as a beautiful shade tree, and for a peculiar mat-like texture which incases it, and which has various mechanical applications.

Nothing that grows has, to my view, such an air of tropical luxuriance as the banana plant, in its different varieties, having immense graceful leaves of a bright-green color, and it is of rapid growth. A large and coarse variety of the fruit takes the place of bread for almost the entire population, eaten boiled or roasted; and a smaller and more delicate kind is a most luscious fruit. The kind which serves as the ordinary food of the laboring masses is cultivated in large fields, which produce extensively with but little culture. A field of the banana plants, with the heavy pendant bunches of the fruit, is the best display of profusion in tropical production.

The wild orange and lemon trees, now laden with fruit, are beautiful objects as the fruit shines among the dark-green leaves; but the oranges are too sour to be agreeable.

Guava trees are abundant, and the fruit is now ripe and ready for making the popular jelly and marmalade. The fruit is sweet and has a rich but not very attractive flavor, and a surfeit of them can soon be attained. I gathered to-day ripe tamarinds, riding under the now leafless trees.

An esculent, which is very productive, and forms a considerable portion of the laborer's diet, is the sweet potato. It is reputed to be better than the sweet potato in the North, but it is, in my opinion, not near so good, being more insipid, heavy, and solid.

The great deficiency in diet for the masses of the people is in regard to fresh meat, its place being poorly supplied by the salted and dried

article. Cattle look pretty well in the fields, and
there seems to be abundant provender for them.
Sheep do not thrive so well; they are thin, and
their wool is very scant and coarse.

The animal which seems the most degenerate
under climatic or other influences, whatever they
may be, is the hog. A Chester County farmer
would not recognize in them the animal which he
has bred up to such perfection. They have long
legs and longer snouts, and are singularly flat
and thin. Taking a front and rear look at them,
they are so narrow as to be almost invisible, but
on broadside view, they make a wonderful slab-
sided display. They must be specially constructed to work their way through the thick
undergrowth in the woods. They are black, and
almost minus bristles. I first saw some of them
in the forest, and thought at a distance that they
were wild goats; but the familiar grunt saved the
life of at least one of them, and avoided another
buzzard inquest.

Nevertheless I can attest that they make good

meat with a somewhat gamy flavor; and they certainly look more like game than gammon.

I had supposed that in this region of endless summer the grazing animals would be harassed by insect annoyances, but it seems not at any seasons to be so much the case as in the North. During my observation not a fly has been seen on horses or oxen, and even the ordinary domestic fly seems to be scarce. When I first noticed the practice of plaiting horses' tails and tying the end to the saddle or girth on one side, it seemed to be a cruelty to restrain the animal from the use of his natural fly-brush, but it is apparently not needed.

I do not notice at this season many insects of any kinds, excepting some varieties of ants, and the evidence of their work, constructive and destructive, is prodigious. The whole country is marked with prominent tumuli which are ant hills. The height of some of these pyramids I have estimated at ten feet. Another kind of ant inhabits a nest which is a large mass, from two to three feet in diameter, fastened on trees, and it is often very destructive when it secures a lodg-ment in the woodwork of houses, reducing the strong framework to a crumbling mass.

Wednesday, March 20th.—I have returned from a long ride, and am impressed with the merits of the Cuban horse. He is a pony-built horse, of

CUBAN HORSE.

good form and capable of long journeys with endurance, but his great merit is his gait as a saddle-horse. The movement is a rack, all horses used under the saddle being trained to it, and long journeys can be accomplished with-out fatigue to the rider. The saddles are large and cumbersome, well suited for novices in riding to keep their position by the hollowness of the seat and by holding on with their hands, but

they seem awkward and inconvenient to experienced riders.

There is some attention given to the stock
and training of these horses, and, among the
better class of people, they are objects of pride
and are well cared for, but I have seen the
saddest abuse of them among a low class of
people in the cities.

When this island, so blessed by nature and
so oppressed by misrule, shall become linked
with our own country, one of the first humane
enactments should be for the prevention of
cruelty to animals. Every traveler here will be
impressed with the great disproportion of the
size and strength of the animal to the amount
of labor required. The horses are mere ponies
in form, but are spurred and beaten to excessive
struggles to move their burdens. They are thin
and jaded, scarred and haggard-looking, and
although naturally of great spirit, their heads
droop to their knees as soon as the burden is removed and the lash ceases its work. In the city
of Havana it is wonderful what these poor beasts

can be made to struggle through under the stimulus of the spur and lash. The spur used is capable of penetrating the flesh, and the heavy clubbed handle of the whip is the favorite end for use. And after such a toilworn existence is near its end, the horse may be sold for a few dollars, to be ridden blindfolded and under goading spurs into the bull-ring to be gored to death; for with only such horses is the wretched bull-fight supplied.

Such is the style of horse and the character of his treatment among the lower classes of the people in Cuban cities; and other animals, as the ox, are liable to similar abuse. I have often seen the yoked ox urged forward by one person pulling on a rope attached to a ring through his nose, while another goaded him in the flanks with a pole tipped at one end with a sharp iron point.

We have a new sensation on this plantation in the arrival of a lot of Chinese laborers, called coolies, just from the vessel, after a voyage of nearly five months. They came to labor under contract for eight years, receiving, beyond their living, the remarkably low wages of four dollars a month.

They look remarkably neat, in dress of Chinese style, with hair in a long plaited tail. They have rather dull, submissive faces, and their smiles are, as is reputed, "childlike and bland." They are rather slightly formed, and, with their small hands and feet, with long finger-nails, I have been wondering what kind of occupation they have been accustomed to at home. It will take some time to inure them to the hard labor they are destined for.

Some of them are weak and sick, due probably to scurvy produced by the privations of their long voyage; but they seem happy, and are greeted by a number of their countrymen who have served for some years on this place.

Their condition here will be, while under contract, but little better than that of the negro slaves with whom they will labor and associate, and they will be subject to the same compulsions and punishments of the lash or stocks, at the mercy of their employers.

Every plantation has a number of coolie laborers, and the importation of them will probably increase with the demand for them. They will take the place of the negro, whose condition of slavery will soon be over, as by government enactment of a few years ago all are born free, and it is the experience here that the freed negro will not labor. I have visited the great plantations, such as Santa Rita, with its nine hundred laborers, and Flor de Cuba, Tinguaro, and others, and have seen large numbers of these coolies. They are preferred for all kinds of skilled labor, but do not bear field work in the hot sun so well as the negro.

I saw, while riding through this cane country this morning, a party hunting a runaway slave. They were mounted, armed with swords and guns, and had with them the traditional Cuban bloodhounds, tied with long cords to their saddles. Instances of slaves running away, occasionally occur, and it is remarkable that they are not more frequent, considering the fact that the runaway can so easily find concealment, and sustain himself on the wild products of the country.

7

Sunday, March 24th.—Yesterday morning we started early with a volante and saddle-horses for a visit to the fine plantation of Tinguaro. The morning was bright, as every morning is, and the air cool as it ever is before the sun's rays get much elevated above the horizon. After a few miles ride through the country of red soil, rais-ing clouds of dust, a great change was experi-enced in reaching a region of the black land, and the marked difference in the soil characteristics was disagreeably manifest. The transition to the black land was rapid, and instead of its being dry and dusty, the mere surface was somewhat dried, and the depth a stiff plastic kind of mud, the roads having deep ruts through which only teams of three yokes of oxen could drag the loads, and the volante had to seek ways which avoided the traveled roads. Yet no rain had fallen for some weeks, the soil retaining moisture so as to form a sticky mud, which is long in drying, and is a great impediment to the operations of the planter. The dark soil is, however, more productive than the red, which is more liable to suffer from drought, but is more readily tilled.

The productive qualities of both soils for some plants is wonderful. I have been informed that there are instances of successive crops of sugar-cane having been taken from fields uninterrupt-edly through a period of forty years, and without the application of manure. Such cropping for fifteen or twenty years is usual.

After reaching Tinguaro, and accepting the in-variable hospitality of the planter, the beautiful plantation of Flor de Cuba, with its fine porti-coed mansion and gorgeous tropical garden, was visited, and gave us great pleasure, and then I took my departure for a tour along the south coast of the island.

The railway travel to Cienfuegos was a hot and dusty ride through a country of no particular attractions. It was varied, but in an uninterest-ing way, by crossing some desert savannas, pro-ducing little more vegetation than the palmetto, which flourishes on the poorest soil. Over these dry and parched soils the air seemed like the

sirocco of an African desert, and water, at least
for drinking purposes, was as scant as there; but
rum could be had, and was in demand, at every
station.

As we passed through some regions the grass
and undergrowth were on fire, and heat and
smoke were added to the already stifling air. The
breeze died out as the afternoon passed, the palmettos did not shake a leaf, and my fellow-travel-
ers smoked and dozed, and dozed and smoked
again. Some fruit-sellers came up to the train,
and the fresh and juicy oranges were refreshing.

I noticed at a station that some of the railroad
timber was mahogany, a useful application of that
usually only ornamental wood. I felt a home-
like sympathy with the engine, bearing the name
of a Philadelphia maker, and with a sharp-vis-
aged, restless-looking Yankee who managed it.

Some fine plantations were passed, but most of
the regions seemed sparsely occupied by people
living in small houses built of bamboo, plastered
with mud, and with roofs thatched with palm
leaves.

The misty hills and the blue waters of the bay of Cienfuegos came in sight as the sun went down, and I breathed the warm soft air from the south coast sea.

In the "Hotel La Union" I found rest in the heavily walled rooms, closed during mid-day from the burning sun, and open from floor to ceiling at night. The hotel is the neatest I have seen on the island, and the fare less *outré* to my taste. There is an air of stiffness about the place, caused by the extraordinary use of starch; for I sit down to a starched table-cloth which crackles on approaching the table; crawl into starched and rustling sheets on the beds ;—even the napkins and towels are rigid, and I am informed that the laundress always starches the pocket-handkerchiefs.

I went this morning to the Plaza, being attracted in that direction by the bell of the old cathedral, and saw the faithful going into the church. The old bell tolled sonorously and solemnly, but soon a very small bell in the same belfry joined in, and made a most discordant clatter.

7*

In the street in front and at the door of the cathedral were rows of music-stands, and a military band came up, and played some beautiful operatic selections, and I sat on the steps, enjoying at least this part of the religious ceremonies. After this was over the band entered the church, and I sat observing with curious interest the varied styles, ranks, castes, and colors of people as they arrived. The ladies came with bare heads, or were covered with veils, and many were followed by servants who carried chairs for them to sit on, and also handsome rugs to kneel on.

The day is Palm Sunday, and some unusual performances, including an abundant display and distribution of palm branches are in order; but besides the religious display the day has not the air of a Sabbath, for business goes on as usual, and some laborers are engaged in repairing the street, even in front of the church.

Within the church the congregation were generally standing or kneeling, and I walked around looking at the paintings and the stained glass of

the windows. People were mingled miscellane-
ously in their worship, and I was impressed with
the extremes of complexion — very dark white
people and very light negroes—and came to the
conclusion that color alone will not go very far
in the distinctions of races on this island.

The practice of whitening the face with cos-
metic powder is universal among the ladies, and
I noticed it abundantly applied on the faces of
very little girls. It was so excessively smeared
in some instances as to be accumulated in masses
in their ears, corners of the mouth, and folds of
skin on the neck and face. But there were many
beautiful faces among the ladies, even after allow-
ing a heavy discount for the cosmetics—certainly
to those who can appreciate the poetry of a face
of waxen pallor, with dreamy, languishing eyes,
and a profusion of drooping black tresses.

There was much ceremonious performance in
the church, which was led off by a fat priest, who
perspired profusely under his exertions and the
burden of his robes. One of the devotees offered
me a piece of palm leaf, which I accepted without

any increase of devotional feeling, and I strolled off, ruminating on the antithesis of religion as a faith and religion as a life practice—on creeds *versus* conduct.

I noticed some doves flying about the old cathedral, lodging on the cornices and belfry, and they seemed at home; but as emblems of peace, humility, and simplicity, with their plain attire, they looked out of place, and I thought how much more appropriately they might be sheltering under the eaves of our old Arch Street Meeting-house. They were, however, well offset by the buzzards, which grovelled in and wrangled for the offal in the street.

My repose last night was broken regularly every hour by a watchman, who bawled out, in a drawling and melancholy manner, immediately under my window, the hour of the night and the character of the weather, information well enough for those who desire to be so informed with that frequency, but I thought it not of sufficient importance to compensate for the loss of the night's rest. I intend for to-night to bribe him into a sin of omission, or to try it on those whose slumbers or potations are deeper than mine. These watchmen are curiously preserved relics of antiquity, going about the streets at night with a long spear in one hand and a lantern in the

WATCHMAN.

other, and making night hideous with their moaning cry. As the weather is so generally clear, their usual cry is *Sereno!* and they are in derision called *Serenos.*

The weather is extremely hot, and the south wind, although it blows strongly from over the bay and the near open sea, is not refreshing. The people have a wilted look, as if oppressed by the heat. Among the lower classes, black and white, the small children go about entirely naked.

The hotel "La Union" is probably one of the best on the island; but this is no great commendation where hotels are uniformly bad. Mr. Trollope, in an article commenting on hotels in general, says that: "The worst hotels that I know are in Havana; nothing can beat them in filth, discomfort, habits of abomination, and absence of everything which the traveler desires."

The hotels of Cuba are all deficient not only in the essentials of comfort for the traveler, but most especially in those of decency and propriety. I found my bed a piece of canvas, tensely stretched, and with merely a starched linen sheet upon it; but I asked for and obtained a blanket, not for covering, but to lie upon. I have occasionally noticed travelers carrying with them heavy rugs, intended to be placed on the hard sacking-bottoms. It is said, in extenuation of the comfortless beds and bare stone or

tiled floors, that mattresses and carpets would
harbor fleas; but that the present arrangements
do not secure an immunity from them every traveler in Cuba will attest.

The manner in which Cuban hotels are built,
with the doors and windows of lodging-rooms
opening on an inclosed area in which all the disagreeable and dirty work is performed, in an entirely exposed manner, renders them unpleasant
to travelers. The view and odor of cooking are
always prominent. As you step from your room
in the morning, it is to see a dirty fellow wring-
ing the necks or plucking the feathers of chickens,
or cleaning fish for your breakfast. The cost of
living in this style, or absence of style, is about
that of really first-class hotels in the North.

The table is excellently supplied with what are
considered delicacies. Oysters are abundant, but
are extremely small, such as would not be gathered in the North; but they have a good flavor.
Coffee served early in the mornings came in
an ordinary glass goblet. Wine of fair quality,
even at the humblest hotels, is supplied without

extra charge. Notwithstanding the abundance of wines and spirits, drunkenness is rare among the native population.

The great number of volantes and other forms of vehicles is characteristic of Cuban cities, but in Cienfuegos they seem scarce.

Wednesday, March 27th.—I took the cars from Cienfuegos for the more agreeable climate of the elevated interior, and arrived at the ancient city of Villa Clara last evening. Part of the way was through regions where the guava trees reached for miles, and where the confections of it are made. At Esperanza, a village noted for its guava jelly and paste, large quantities were seen and offered for sale in the cars. There were several different kinds, and all were delightful and superior to any I had heretofore tasted.

It seemed out of time to be gathering crops of Indian corn, as I noticed on the way, in the glowing verdure of these latter days of a tropical March; but the stalks and blades were withered, and the fields reminded me of home-days in October. Two crops of corn are raised in the year.

During the route we have had in view, to the eastward, some ranges of mountains, and have been surprised at a curious illusion as to their distance. Some guesses located them as near as three miles, but they were actually from forty to sixty miles away.

Villa Clara looks like an old Moorish city, and here may be seen the purest types of Cuban people. It does not seem to have a business character, but there is evidence of wealth among the citizens. I should think that the population is mostly made up of wealthy and retired planters.

I was attracted in the evening by a band of music on the Plaza, and on reaching it, was surprised to find such an ornamental promenade, large, and brightly lighted with gas, which, with the more romantic illumination of a full moon, shining on light stone buildings and through heavy foliage, made it a kind of fairy-land spectacle. While the band played in the centre, a large number of prettily dressed ladies promenaded around the enclosure, and as Villa Clara is noted in song and story for its beautiful ladies, I took the opportunity of verifying the fact.

Hotels here are of humble character, but with grandiloquent names. I lodged at the Hotel "La Cinque Villas," and would have slept but for another noisy peripatetic watchman, who lugubriously stated that the weather was cloudy, in which information I was previously posted by rain pattering on the tiled roof above me.

It is evident that people do not travel much on this island; the cars are not well filled, particularly the first class cars, and there are but one or two trains a day, even on the most traveled roads. Before the days of railroads there could not have been any active intercommunication, on account of the bad quality of the common roads. For this reason a vast proportion of the masses of the people have seen but little beyond their immediate vicinity.

At this dry season the roads in the level country are good; but the difficulty is after rains, when they become impassable to vehicles on account of the depth of the mud. The wheels sink to the axle, and the sticky mud adheres until spokes and rim are hidden in one mass.   This is truly a land of mud in the wet season, and I have heard in Spanish the exaggerated expression, that " the roads become so muddy that a bird cannot fly over them."

It does not seem possible that even the most traveled roads can be constructed to remain good during the wet season, on account of the scarcity of timber and hard stone.

The quaint-looking volante, with its enormous wheels, has some merit for dragging through these roads when three horses are geared to it abreast, one being ridden by a driver who urges them on.   But this vehicular oddity will soon disappear or will be retained merely as a conventionality of style for a nobby family equipage.

Saturday, March 30th.—I engaged a volante driver, who, by the way, stated that his name was "Jesus of Mary," to rouse me for the early train westward yesterday morning, and, ere the dawn, he shouted between the bars of the lodging-room. After groping for some time, a pint of water was found, which my friend and I divided between us for our ablutions, and we left this comfortless inn without even the offering of a morning draught of coffee. Thence we journeyed to the plantation of Tinguaro, and, after a welcome from its hospitable household, mounted saddle horses, and nightfall found us in the sociality of home life on the plantation of Santa Barbara.

The sensation of this morning is the melancholy announcement that one of the newly arrived Chinese laborers was found dead, having committed suicide by hanging himself to a beam across the bathing-house. The self-murder was effected in a determined manner, as the feet were almost touching the floor, a ledge was within their reach, and objects of support could have been readily seized by the hands. Suicide has been of frequent occurrence among the coolies in Cuba, and the practice has often been followed by imitation of their associates. Sometimes it seems to have been accomplished in a spirit of vindictiveness towards their employers, and, again, in a curious belief of their transmigration

back to China after death. I have been informed
that on one estate, after several single suicides,
six coolies were found on one morning hanging by
the neck. It is said that further instances were
prevented by making in the presence of their com-
rades a complete dissection and mutilation of one
of the bodies. With a similar object, the bodies
in some cases of suicide were placed on a pile of
wood and totally destroyed by fire. These horrible sights, it is said, took from the Chinese
their romantic ideas on the subject of self-de-
struction.

The Chinese laborers are of mild and tractable temperament, seem to be contented with
their humble duties, and are submissive to the
abuse to which they are on some plantations sub-
jected; but when once their revengeful nature is
aroused, they mutually combine with each other
and have proved dangerous in their rage. I saw
yesterday an officer of a plantation whose arm
had been severed in an attack, and in another
neighborhood a white employer was murdered
by them, his skull having been hacked to pieces

by their hoes, each one of the infuriated coolies striking a blow at him.

The body of the Chinese suicide has been interred outside the walls of the little enclosure which, by church regulation, must receive the remains of those only who have been baptized in the Catholic faith. In digging the shallow grave to receive the body, another sleeper was unceremoniously turned out by the spades, and I saw the decaying remnants of mortality, including a skull with some matted hair and portions of clothing, scattered on the ground, and they were left so to remain. Such disregard of propriety in regard to the repose of the dead is the custom throughout the island. The poorer classes are buried without coffins, just beneath the surface, and the bodies quickly decay in the perpetually heated earth.

Monday, April 1st.—At sunrise this morning the volante and saddle-horses were ready for a ride of a few leagues to Colon, one of the more modern of Cuban inland towns. It seems to be the first place in the island to bear the name of its great discoverer. In the name of Cristobal Colon we seem hardly able to recognize its Latinized and, to us, familiar rendering of Christopher Columbus.

I felt curious to know whether these old-fashioned people would build a new town after the quaint and semi-barbaric styles of the old, but was gratified to find some evidences of progress. The streets were wide and regularly laid out. In some of the old Moorish-styled towns of the island, it would not be a very long leap to cross the street by jumping from the projecting eaves of the roof on one side to those on the other. There is also the modern improvement of side-walks to the streets, which they have actually gotten .wide enough· for two persons to walk together. The pavements are edged and shaded by long and beautiful rows of laurel trees.

An ornamental plaza, the inevitable pleasure resort of every Cuban town, is being laid out, and I took some interest in watching the progress of building a cathedral, which will be large, but not grand. The work was crawling along in

the usual national style. Some coolies and negroes were removing a heap of gravel at the
building by putting it into small boxes and placing them on their heads. They then slowly
walked off with them, emptied the contents, and
returned to the heap. A man with a large whip,
in slave-driver style, superintended the work.
I pictured to myself, by way of comparison, a
smart Irishman, with spade and wheelbarrow, at
that gravel heap, doing in less time the work of
the dozen laborers, and not requiring an extra
hand to wield the lash.

At a farrier's shop in the vicinity I noticed
that it required three men to shoe a horse, one to
do the work while another held the hoof, and the
third held the horse's head and gave general as-
sistance; yet withal the work progressed slowly.

The streets are macadamized with white stone,
and the glare from them and from the light-
colored houses was intolerable under the vertical
sun of mid-day.

A visit to the prison was interesting, and a
keeper courteously showed the interior. The

prisoners were mostly coolies and negroes, and were employed in braiding palm-leaves for hats, and in making cigarettes. The garrote was an object of grim interest. The keeper apologized for its being dirty and out of order, that it had not been used very lately. My attention was attracted to some rudely made, high-backed chairs, the use of which was explained to be, "to seat the dead ones upon before the spectators, to make room for others on the garroting stool!"

NEGRO HUT.

Wednesday, April 3d.—We have to-day journeyed from the interior of the island to Havana;

from the fresh air of the country, with cool nights and breezy noons, to the unvarying heat, dust, and close air of the city. The course has been through varied regions, from the level cane-fields and the farm lands to the fruit groves and gardens near the metropolis. The view was over a country mostly level, but it was on the north side terminated by a distant mountain range, or by the hills bordering the north coast. Many of the most attractive towns were passed through, and near Havana were to be seen palatial villas, romantically located on eminences, the brilliant contrast of their blue, yellow, and white colors with the light and dark-tinted foliage being beautifully effective. The general adoption of blue as a part of the color of buildings gives a picturesqe addition to the landscape.

After a brief experience of the Hotel el Telegrafo, I am inclined to recant at least some of my anathemas against Cuban hotels in general. Some of the abominations so conspicuous in the court-yard enclosures are here partially hidden by a conservatory of flowers, in the form of a

EL PASEO DE ISABEL.

garden, on the tiled roof of a low building that almost fills the space; but there is the same tendency to the accumulation of empty boxes, barrels, and trash in corners, and there are offensive adjuncts that diffuse horrible odors. The fare at the table is really good and free from the disgusting qualities of garlic and oiliness, which is a relief after a few weeks' feeding on the usual fare everywhere in Cuba. In commending the fare in general, it is not necessary to except the article of butter, for that will never be even tasted by the traveler anywhere on the island, as its rancid odor is sufficiently diffused to be a safe precaution.

Some of the rooms at this hotel are little en-closures, singularly but advantageously located on the roof, and they have decided merits with regard to ventilation. About them there is a spacious promenade on the level roof, enclosed within battlement-walls, and its elevation gives a good lookout over the city and surroundings. It also gives to the curious observer an opportunity of prying into the customs and doings of our neighbors, one of whom, I notice, keeps his goats on an adjoining roof; and on another tiled roof is a horse enjoying high life in that unstable position.

I have been interested in observing the remnants of the massive ancient walls which once

OLD CITY WALLS.

enclosed and, in their day, strongly fortified the city of Havana; but the town has long since outgrown its enclosure, and the outlines of the walls mark but an oblong section of the centre of the city. Building and street improvements have generally removed the walls, but enough remain for objects of curiosity and interest as ruins.

One of the great entrances of the city, called the
Tierra Gate, which is architecturally ornamental,

TIERRA GATE.

still remains. I noticed in one place that the
keeper of a monkey-show had made an excavation
in a part of the wall, leaving its exterior but a
hollow shell, and was peacefully amusing the people; to such base uses had it come at last.

The remains of Columbus lie in the ancient
cathedral of Havana. If there is a tomb at which

homage is due, it is that of the man who, dis-
covering a world, received naught but insult and
sorrow as his earthly reward, and to whose honor
small tribute has since been paid. The remains
of Columbus, after the third removal, were finally
deposited in a metallic box, which is now encased

TOMB OF COLUMBUS.

in the masonry at the side of the altar of this old
church. Some years after his death his ashes
were removed from Spain to the island of St.
Domingo, and about seventy-five years ago they

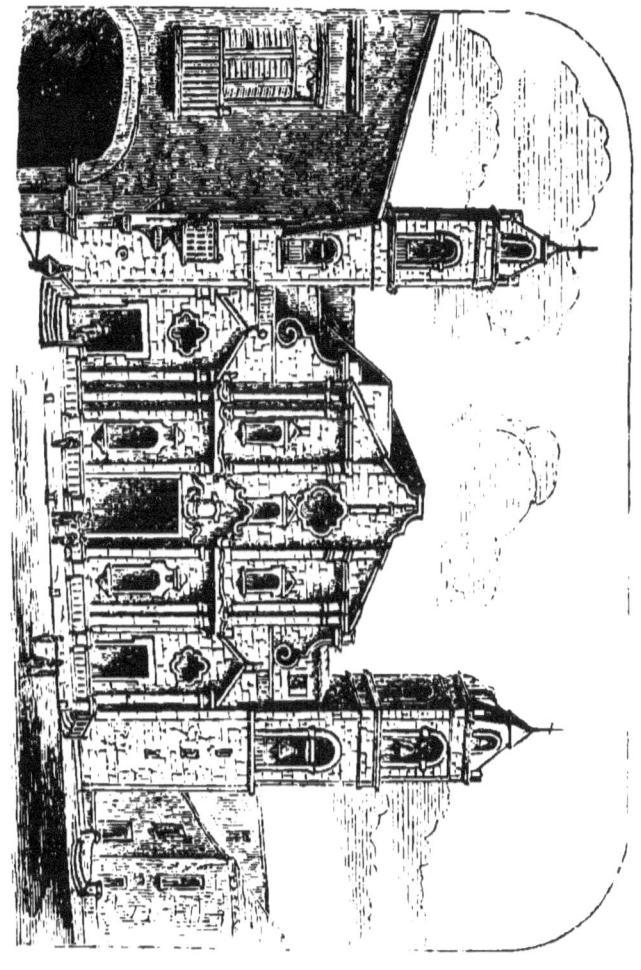

CATHEDRAL OF HAVANA.

9*

were brought to Havana. I have been informed that when disinterred for the last time, which was nearly three hundred years after his death, but little of even dust was found, and but one bone. A tablet in the wall, and a bust of the great discoverer, upon which some unworthy lines of commonplace sentiment are inscribed, are all that indicate the tomb.

The cathedral was built about one hundred and fifty years ago, and, besides its being honored as the mausoleum of Columbus, is interesting on account of its great size and quaint architecture. It is constructed of coral limestone, originally white, but now dingy from age, and I noticed the arborescent tracings of coral branches and shell impressions on every stone within reach of the eye.

The building was closed when I reached it, but curiosity led me to grope around a yard in its rear, where I found a man who held a bunch of keys in his hand, and some small coins caused those keys to grate musically in the rusty locks which led through recesses dark and mysterious, until the inner temple was gained. A "dim religious light" was cast over the sculpture, paintings, and on the grand mosaic floors, and two perpetually burning tapers in large vases of oil glowed faintly on the altar.

I had reached the heart of the man with the keys, and he continued to invade for me the sacerdotal privacies of gorgeous priestly robes, and showed all the costly machinery of religion, in pure gold and silver, including the paraphernalia of parades, locked up in great mahogany chests and closets.

What a chance here for sacrilegious plunder may some day come, should anarchy precede this island's political day of reckoning and redemption from bondage!

The very name Havana is so associated with cigars that visitors are curious to see something of their production, and knowing that the great cigarette factory of " La Honradez " is courteously open for inspection, we saw the manner in which more than two millions of cigarettes are made every day, mostly by the labor of Chinese operatives, who have acquired great dexterity in the manipulations. There is a large amount of fine and ingenious machinery in the establishment, which, I notice, bears the name of American manufacturers; and indeed it is elsewhere, as here, on this island, that all that represents ingenuity, invention, and the progress of intelligence, may be referred for its origin either to the United States or England.

I have never been in any locality, from the capital to the most obscure village, where the lottery-ticket venders are not noisy annoyances and disagreeable importuners. They are seen in every public place, press the stranger in the hotels, at railway stations, and in the streets, and are indeed scarcely ever out of sight where people are passing or are congregated. The ticket-sellers are of all ages, from children to the old and decrepit.

The lottery is under government patronage; a large revenue being derived from it, as one-fourth of the amount of the money staked is appropriated by the state. It is therefore the wretched policy to encourage the demoralizing institution, to the great injury of the people, as it appears that few in the community avoid yielding to the temptation to "try their luck."

The successful drawings are publicly announced, and thus the cupidity of persons is kept excited by hearing of money in great sums, as from one to three hundred thousand dollars, being drawn.

The number of persons who continually invest all above a bare subsistence in these schemes, and still keep hoping on for a chance fortune, must be very great. The few successes are loudly proclaimed, while the vast number of blanks is forgotten; but a sure prize every time, is to the government which withholds its proportion of the capital as revenue.

Friday, April 5th.—The botanical gardens, located in the suburbs of Havana, are beautiful beyond any gardens I have ever seen, and exceeded my anticipations of them. Indeed the place is such as might have formed the fabric of a dream of Oriental romance, or of an Arabian night's tale. Tropical foliage, flowers, groves, streams, and fountains make it up—all too much of beauty for description.

After leaving the gardens, we rode in the volante to the top of a great hill which overlooks the city and surroundings, and over the blue expanse of the Gulf of Mexico. The hill slopes down in a single declivity to where the white surf marks a line between the grassy verdure and the blue water.

On this hill is an object which is a sad transition from the blooming gardens below,—the cemetery in which the dead of the poorer classes are deposited. Here are pits in which the uncoffined bodies are piled, one upon another, and over each is strewn a little lime and earth, until the surface is nearly reached, when all is made level over it, and another pit is dug, to be in the same manner filled. I have been informed that bodies are sometimes brought to the ground in coffins in which the bottom is arranged on hinges so as to drop its occupant into the pit. When the bodies come with clothing on, it is said to be the custom to first mutilate the garments and render them useless, so that they may not be stolen.

In another cemetery, located near the Gulf shore, are deposited the bodies of those who have not died in the faith of priestcraft, and are not privileged to repose in holy ground. Here the space for burial is so limited that the defunct have even but a temporary occupancy of their

CUBAN TOMBS.

charnel-house, and a new incumbent cannot be deposited without turning out previous occupants. As a consequence, therefore, the ground is strewn with the bleaching relics of mortality, and in one corner is a heap, mostly of skulls, several yards high.

I visited another cemetery, or rather a great mausoleum, where the bodies of those whose faith and pockets are both deep, are deposited. It consists of courses of masonry, above ground, in which are left caverns like baker's ovens or large pigeon-holes, each of sufficient size to hold two or three coffins. When a body is placed in one of them, the end is sealed up with a slab on which is inscribed the name of the deceased. When I saw these mural abodes of the dead, the walls were heated under the burning sun, and I thought of the thousand or more dead bodies within, undergoing a process little short of cremation.

The most popular amusements in this country are those which depend for their interest on the sufferings inflicted on animals. The most universal amusement of this character, prevailing throughout the small towns of the interior as well as in the cities, is cockfighting, evidence of which, in the raising and trading in game-cocks, is continually observed. They are seen in all regions,

10

carried about in a kind of cage or basket woven from the palm-leaf, so constructed that the heads and necks of the chickens project through an opening in the top. There is a wretched practice of plucking out the feathers from their bodies, excepting the wings and tail, inducing, of course, suffering in the operation, and a painful exposure of the tender skin. I suppose that the battles are purposely fought in this nude state to add to the severity of wounds, and, therefore, to the enjoyment of the spectators.

The amusement which would in these times disgrace even the most barbaric horde, and which lacks every vestige of manliness in sport, is the so-called bull-fight. It is not entitled to the name of a fight, which would imply a combat involving two sides more or less matched, but is the torturing of a bull into frenzy, to escape or to wound aged, dilapidated, and enfeebled horses, who are blindfolded so that they cannot avoid receiving injury.

I have not witnessed this amusement of torturing a bull and mangling horses, but know its

horrors from those who have lately been present
at it. The bull is irritated by smarting wounds
before he is brought into the arena, and if not
infuriated enough, his skin is pricked with barbed
darts that remain in the flesh. Should his struggles not be sufficiently exciting to the crowd,
burning fuses are added to the darts. He is also
wounded by the spear of the rider who is mounted
on the miserable horse. The horse is at length

LANCER.

disabled by the horns of the bull, or he may be
killed outright. I have been informed, that when
the abdomen of the horse happens to be ripped
open so that the bowels protrude and trail in the
dust, the rent is roughly sewed up, and the poor

beast is spurred on to endure still greater suffering.

To the credit of humanity be it told, this horrible show is declining, and that it is now merely attended by the lower classes of the community, and that women are not usually present; but the continued national recognition of the abomination is evinced by a bull-fight having been gotten up by the authorities to entertain the Russian Prince at his recent visit. It is also proper here to state that these authorities are native Spaniards, and not Cubans.

This " Ever Faithful Isle" will remain faithful just so long as the present powerful military government can continue its authority. The people are held in subjection by a large Spanish army, and by a perfect military system which is spread over the island.

The entire governing power is in the hands of the Spaniards, the native Cubans being excluded from military appointments or offices under the government.

The people are ready and anxious for relief

from the tyranny of Spain; but there seems to be now but little hope for, and apparently no general sympathy with the rebellion, which has been in existence for several years at the eastern end of the island, and which does not, and probably has never acted as an organized force. The hatred of the Cubans against their Spanish rulers is extreme; however subdued may be its appearance under military subjection, I know from intimate communication with the people its heartfelt intensity.

Soldiers are almost ever in sight in all localities, city and rural, and the Cubans are severely taxed for the support of this proportionately great standing army.

The hope for relief of the Cubans must, I think, come from liberal and enlightened nations abroad, and they will, at the proper time, patriotically sacrifice life and property in a hopeful effort for release. Their course is to be commended to all friends of liberality and human progress.

Monday, April 8th.—As a winter resort for

invalids of a certain class, the merits of Cuba have long been recognized, and with the increase of domestic comforts for health and pleasure-seekers, and the improvement of facilities for traveling, the time may soon come when the flight of valetudinarians to escape the severity of northern winters will be generally to the genial climate of this island. The climate is probably more faultless than that of any locality at an equal distance from northern homes, for the avoidance of coldness and rapid transitions of temperature, particularly if proper locations on the island be selected.

The south coast of Cuba has the advantage of being protected by the mountain ranges from the north winds, which occasionally prevail for a day or two at a time, and are the cause of the only marked depressions of temperature. Besides the rural localities on that coast, the best resort, and that which is most frequented by invalids, is the city of Trinidad. Other cities of the south of Cuba are not so well located as to the hygienic influences in and about them, and they are subject to malarial taints, to which foreigners are very susceptible, and even yellow fever, during some winters, continues to prevail in them to a limited extent.

Locations on the north coast, or its vicinity, are too much under the influence of changes produced by north winds, for the secure residence of impressible invalids.

From observation of the hygienic conditions of Cuban cities in general, I would, however, advise invalids to avoid them all, and to resort for permanency of stay, to the villages or rural localities of the interior. Havana has, far beyond other cities of Cuba, its comforts, conveniences, social attractions, and amusements, for the advantage of residence for invalids; but the temperature, while it is liable to sudden northern influences, is apt to be too high for comfort during most of the time, and the city is scarcely ever absolutely free from cases of yellow fever. The causes of yellow fever seem to exist always in the vicinity of the harbor, and during my short stay, I know that there have been five cases of this terrible disease in one popular hotel in such proximity; and it should be borne in mind that foreigners, as in the above instances, are usually the victims.

The harbors on which the largest Cuban cities are located are almost landlocked, tideless basins, without a current washing through them; and as they receive the entire surface drainage and sewage, the waters become foul and liable to engender pestilence.

These unfavorable conditions pertain especially to the harbor of Havana, the water of which is so foul that, as a naval officer informed me, even the washing of the decks of vessels with it is avoided, and that when an anchor is raised from the bottom the adherent mud has a most intolerable and sickening stench. A plan has been projected for producing a current through the harbor by cutting a canal from its upper extremity across the narrow strip intervening between it and the shore of the Gulf of Mexico. Should the project be successfully accomplished, it will undoubtedly have a favorable influence on the salubrity of the city

Invalids frequently resort to certain baths and mineral springs in Cuba, which have a traditional, but, I think, a dubious reputation, as specific in certain diseases; and the climate of the Isle of Pines, which is about fifty miles south from this island, is claimed to be remarkably bland and free from vicissitudes, and patients with bronchial affections are said to be well suited by it.

The want of good accommodations and the subjection to unavoidable annoyances are the drawbacks to such places. The diet that is offered may not be endurable to the fastidious invalid, hard beds may not permit his repose, and fleas and mosquitoes may be the climax of his miseries.

The cold, earnest North is the land of labor, and this is the land of idleness and ease. That Cuba has produced nought of value in literature, and added nothing to science, may be attributed to climatic influences. All who come here from the stimulating atmosphere of the hard-working North soon yield to a sense of ease and tranquillity as "the South's soft languor o'er their senses steals."

It is the climate for the overworked and the care-worn; for the many in whom the nervous system is strung to morbid tension until its vibrations are painful; for all who, weary with the battle of life, would seek for rest from the stimulus of their own excitability. It is the place for an idle, dreamy existence, and labor here is only done under dire necessity, or by an inferior race under compulsion of the lash.

To breakfast at eleven in the morning and then to retire for a nap would, in the North, give the idea of the intensity of laziness; yet such is the general custom, and Northern sojourners take very kindly to the easy fashion. My own personal experience is that the lazy ways of the country are easily adopted and followed. It is easy to have the drowsiness of the night shaken off by a cup of hot coffee brought to you as you still recline at sunrise. It is agreeable afterwards to ride on a horse whose movement is so easy that it cannot jolt the sentiment out of you, or

COUNTRY HOUSE.

break the thread of your reverie. Such a ride, not over the stale conventionality of traveled roads, but through untrodden, ever-varying ways, amidst scenery made up of objects new and interesting, while the air is still cool and fresh, is all the exertion that the morning requires. Then follow the hours of idleness and repose, while the sun's rays are burning and almost vertical. The dinner-hour comes as the day declines, and the after hours may be again pleasantly spent in out-door exercise or amusement. In this easy manner time passes away, until the visitor is reluctantly compelled to think of his interests in the severe and earnest North, and begins his preparation for turning away from this land of listlessness and ease.

Mental activity is as little prevalent among the Cubans as is physical. Books are but little seen in the houses of even the higher class, and I have never detected any one in the act of reading. The people, however, are generally bright and intelligent, and they have a suavity of manner and courteous deportment towards each other which

11

give, even among the humblest, an air of culture and refinement above their actual intellectual attainments.

The lives of Cuban ladies must be, according to our Northern ideas, dull and wearisome from ennui and restraint. In the cities, custom prevents their going out unattended, walking seems to be considered vulgar, and their daytime is spent in talking, dozing, and rocking, followed perhaps by a languid evening ride in the volante.

But my Cuban days are at an end. Home thoughts steal in even while I am looking on scenes of interest, and in the burning heat of this city I feel that a cool draft of northern air would be refreshing. In my stroll in the streets last evening, a band of wandering minstrels played the air of "Home, sweet home," and I was unusually impressible to that ever-impressive melody. The approach of our old friend, the steamship "Juniata," was announced by signals on the Morro Castle this morning, and she is now moored in the harbor, ready for her northward course. The meeting with her good commander seemed a harbinger of home. How welcome was the sight of his manly face, glowing warmly with good nature like a tropical sunrise, and in the genial grasp of his hand I felt that a true sailor was spliced fast to me.

Wednesday, April 10*th.*—The time has come at last to turn away our faces from this beautiful land, and we now see the sun set for the last time over the purple hills of Cuba, as the vessel heads northward—homeward bound! What a radiant and glowing tropical sunset scene of sky, sea, and land is spread before us as ends with the day our real visions of the "isle of undying verdure!" A glittering pathway leads over the sea towards the western horizon, and clouds, land, and water are fused in the red and golden tints of parting sunlight.

> "The golden sea its mirror spreads
>   Beneath the golden skies,
> And but a narrow strip between
>   Of land and shadow lies.

" The sea is but another sky,
  The sky a sea as well,
And which is earth and which the heavens,
  The eye can scarcely tell.

" So when for us life's evening hour
  Soft fading shall descend,
May glory, born of earth and heaven,
  The earth and heavens blend."

THE END.

www.ingramcontent.com/pod-product-compliance
Lightning Source LLC
Chambersburg PA
CBHW032016010726
47493CB00007B/2429